Hugo *and the*
Long Red Arm

White Wolves Series Consultant: Sue Ellis,
Centre for Literacy in Primary Education

This book can be used in the White Wolves Guided Reading programme
with children who have an average level of reading experience at Year 4 level

Reprinted 2006
First published 2004 by
A & C Black Publishers Ltd
38 Soho Square, London, W1D 3HB

www.acblack.com

ISBN 0-7136-6840-7
ISBN 978-0-7136-6840-7

A CIP catalogue for this book is available from the British Library.

A & C Black uses paper produced with elemental chlorine-free
pulp, harvested from managed sustained forests.

Printed and bound in Spain by G. Z. Printek, Bilbao.

Hugo and the Long Red Arm

by Rachel Anderson

illustrated by Scoular Anderson

A & C Black • London

For Nguyen Robertson

Contents

Chapter One

The Base Camp at the Top of the Stairs

In Hugo Spoon's near-perfect world, there were two tip-top activities.

One: eating hot baked potatoes.

Two: playing with his Medi-Rescue-Mission-Men.

He did other things too.

He fed the cat. He slept peacefully each night. Several times a day he helped his brother, Aidan, look for his lost shoes.

Every few minutes he rescued a piece of Medi-Rescue-Mission-Men equipment from baby Bella's mouth.

He also ran useful errands for his mother: fetching paper clips, a dowsing-rod, some umbrella spokes, a plastic windmill, a hubcap, or any other bits and pieces that she needed in her workshop.

Among Lillian Spoon's inventions was a solar-powered baby buggy, self-opening curtains, disappearing sticking-plaster, and a paw-operated tin-opener for hungry cats. She was now finishing off the shoe-seeking robot for Aidan.

Hugo's father, Patrick Spoon,
invented vegetarian recipes.
Hugo helped him, too.

Hugo's favourite topping on a
baked potato was crispy-kelp-and-
ginger dressing. His favourite
place for setting up base camp for
the Medi-Rescue-Mission-Men
was on the landing at the top of
the stairs.

One evening, Hugo had just set up a tricky incident for his Medi-Rescue-Mission-Men when he heard the crunch of snapping plastic. Another paramedic's arm was crushed beneath Uncle Harold's big boots.

"Bit old for playing toy soldiers, aren't you, lad?" boomed Uncle Harold.

Hugo clipped a replacement swivel arm into the paramedic's shoulder socket but kept his lips buttoned.

Uncle Harold wanted to be an inventor too, only his ideas, like the singing kettle and the electric toothbrush, had all been invented before. Hugo wished Uncle Harold didn't share their home. But Lillian said, "Custard's thicker than water."

"Hugo!" Patrick called. "Time to lend a hand."

Bother! he thought, because he hadn't finished rescuing his team and he didn't like to leave them in their risky situation.

Lillian came down from her workshop in the attic. She had to step round the rescuers.

"Hugo!" she scolded. "I've told you a trillion times! This is not a sensible place for a base camp. Please move your men off the landing."

"Yes, Mum."

"A grown-up could easily trip over a Mission Man and fall down the stairs."

The entire team of Medi-Rescue-Mission Men nodded in agreement. But it wasn't one of the grown-ups who had the accident. It was Hugo.

Chapter Two

Emergency Stations

As Hugo reached out to save the last of the Medi-Rescue-Mission-Men, the Man swung beyond Hugo's grasp. They both lost their footing. The paramedic landed safely. But Hugo hurtled backwards down the stairs.

His elbow hit the ground first. Then his shoulder. Then the rest. The pain was like fire.

"Poor Hugo. Better soon," said Aidan.

"Glug gloog," said Bella.

"He's very pale," said Lillian.

"Storm in a teacup, if you ask me. The boy's a regular fusspot," said Uncle Harold as he hurried back upstairs with a sly smile.

Hugo's arm was out of shape. "Maybe we'd better not try to fix it ourselves this time," said Patrick.

Lillian agreed. They should let the hospital sort it out.

Accident and Emergency was buzzing. Victims from every type of home disaster were being treated.

A granny had knitted herself inside a stocking.

A baby had swallowed a jar of jellybeans.

A lollipop lady had caught her thumb in her jacket zip.

All were receiving chocolate drops and TLC.

Hugo was the only patient with broken bones so the nurse was very pleased to be able to look after him.

"You choose your own colour for the plaster," he told Hugo. "And today's special offers are nite-glo green or blood-and-thunder red."

Hugo didn't care about colours. "I'll take the red," he said miserably.

So his arm was set in a heavy red cast. Hugo could hardly move it. It felt like a quite separate limb.

Back home, his life was no longer near-perfect. The two worst things were:

First: the pain.

Second: the not-being-able-to-do-anything-for-himself.

"I'm just useless," said Hugo.

"You can say that again!" chuckled Uncle Harold as he helped himself to the biggest baked potato on the dish.

All next day, Hugo lay in the garden with the clumsy cast resting on the cat.

"I hardly slept a wink last night," he moaned. "So there's no point going to school tomorrow. I won't be able to do anything. I wish I was a Medi-Rescue-Mission-Man. Then I'd just click in a new arm."

But Hugo didn't believe in magic. He knew wishes were just words.

Chapter Three

Potions and Pegs

After Hugo had been helped into his sleeping-suit by the cat, had his teeth cleaned for him by Bella and been launched up into his hammock by Aidan, Patrick came along with a glass jug.

"Beddy-byes drink," he said. "Specially for you."

Patrick often mixed unusual potions, such as a teething syrup for Bella and an anti-flea tonic for the cat.

However, he had never invented anything as thick and red as this before. Hugo wondered what was in it.

"Well, I added hops for sound sleep. Spinach for strength. A teaspoonful of moon-sugar. And several other significant things."

Then Lillian brought down her latest invention. She called it a triple-function limb attachment. "To reach, grab or twirl," she said.

It was made from two clothes pegs, four wire coat-hangers, a rechargeable torch battery, six rubber bands, and some disappearing sticking-plaster.

"Wow!" said Hugo. His mother had invented the buggy for Bella, the shoe-searcher for Aidan. But this was the first gadget she'd made specially for him.

"Shall I install it for you?" Lillian asked.

"And would you like to try this yummy potion?" Patrick asked.

Hugo had no time to wonder what the attachment and the potion would do to him before his eyes snapped shut. He slept like a log.

When he woke, he felt ready for anything till he saw his arm.

It reached to the end of his
hammock.

"Aha!" said Lillian. "The
triple-function limb is supposed to
have an exceptionally long reach,
an exceedingly strong grab and an
outstandingly speedy twirl."

At school everybody stared. "Hey, Hugo! Whatever's happened?" they asked. But nobody listened to anybody else because suddenly they were all talking at once.

"My auntie broke her nose playing tiddlywinks."

"My brother broke his arm playing cribbage."

"My dad broke a rib playing dumb crambo."

Since everybody knew somebody who'd broken something, Hugo stopped feeling unusual. However, at playtime, he wasn't allowed outside with the others.

He had to sit in the Quiet Room. Miranda was there too. She'd hidden her glasses again. None of the teachers could find them.

Miranda whispered to Hugo, "They're behind the radiator."

At once, Hugo's arm inside the red cast started to itch.

Chapter Four

Intruder in the Night

The springs quivered. The sticking-plaster rippled, the battery glowed. The triple-function limb slithered forward like a snake across the Quiet Room as far as the radiator. Then it twisted behind the radiator. Then it made its exceedingly strong grab and suddenly, Miranda's glasses were safe in the grip of the clothes pegs. Then they were back on Miranda's nose.

Hugo was highly praised for being so helpful.

But the triple-function limb had a will of its own. It dipped under the desks and with its clothes-peg pincers, knotted chattery Nathalie's plaits to the back of her chair.

During the afternoon, it moved on to the football field, grabbed the ball from the ref and kept it twirling like a planet just above the players' heads. They were furious.

On the way home, it darted into the open mouth of the

pillar box, grabbed the letters, then twirled them high into the air 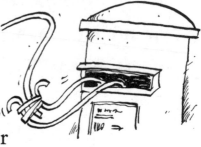 like autumn leaves.

At home, it zoomed across the table, grabbed the biggest potato off the dish and twirled it so fast it turned to mash on the ceiling.

"Manners, manners," muttered Uncle Harold, who'd had his eye on that spud.

Lillian said firmly, "I know it's difficult, Hugo, coping with a broken arm. But please set a good example to Aidan and Bella."

Hugo tried to keep his arm secure in the sling. But the triple-function limb couldn't resist mischief. And it never ever lifted a finger to help any of the Spoons.

In the supermarket, it swept
cheese strings off the shelves and
juggled with Brussels sprouts. At
the park, it threw Bella's dummy
to the ducks, then dug for rabbits
in the sandpit.

While Hugo was sleeping, and couldn't keep an eye on it, the triple-function limb arm got into the most mischief.

At least, Hugo supposed it must be the triple-function limb. Who else would creep about at dead of night to create such trouble?

Then, one night, the scrabbling
was so loud that Hugo woke.

To his surprise, he saw the triple-
function limb lying on the duvet,
quiet as a resting cockroach.

But the noise went on, like
drawers being opened, shelves
tipped over, and cupboards
shaken. And it was coming from
Lillian's workshop, as though
something or somebody was on
the rampage.

It was unsettling. Hugo knew his mother was asleep. He could hear her snoring. Everybody was asleep, even Bella. Or nearly everybody.

Mission-Men, as Hugo knew, should always be ready for whatever task came their way.

But what if it was a burglar?
Armed with a big stick?

Hugo thought he was too scared
to move. But mischief and mayhem
were the lifeblood of the triple-
function limb. It reached out of the
hammock, across the room, on to
the landing, along the passage and
up the stairs towards Lillian's
workshop. Hugo had to go with it.

And there, crouching behind Lillian's workbench, was Uncle Harold. The place was in chaos. It was clear what Uncle Harold was up to. He was searching for something.

"How dare you!" Hugo shouted.

Uncle Harold glanced round. Greed was in his eyes. Guilt was tattooed on his face.

"You sneaky thief!" Hugo yelled. "You've been trying to steal my mum's best ideas, haven't you?"

Lillian's notebooks were flung about, her diagrams crumpled and scattered, her models set free and scuttling up the walls like crazy mice.

"It's not fair, not fair!" Uncle Harold stamped his feet. Under the heavy soles of his hairy-wolf slippers another of Lillian's models was crushed to pieces. "Why does *she* have all the good ideas? I only wanted a few."

Before Hugo had time to run down and fetch Patrick, the clothes-peg pincers had grabbed Uncle Harold by the scruff of his neck. And there was to be no mercy shown.

Chapter Five

Uncle Harold's Comeuppance

Uncle Harold bellowed and struggled. But he was held too tightly to break free. Then the terrible twirling began. Uncle Harold was twirled and twirled like a human catherine wheel till his guilty eyes were popping.

"Put me down or I'll call for the police!" he bawled.

"Tip-top idea!" said Patrick.

"In fact, that's just what my clever wife is doing right now."

Lillian decided to try out the new laser-light alarm. It turned out to be most effective.

Two constables skidded up on their skateboards almost before she'd finished pushing the right buttons.

Uncle Harold was arrested. Tucked into his pyjama pockets and into his string vest were the plans for all Lillian's most interesting inventions.

"Oh, Harold, how *could* you?" Lillian said sadly as Harold was escorted away.

One of the best things about
catching Uncle Harold red-handed
in the act of theft was that Hugo
didn't feel useless any more. He
was such a hero that a woman
came from the newspaper to take
his photo.

Patrick said, "Sorry, madam, but we haven't time to gossip now. We have to go to the fracture clinic for Hugo's next appointment."

So the photographer took Lillian and Aidan and Bella's picture instead as "Family of the Hero".

Lillian was pleased. It gave her a chance to talk about the usefulness of her many inventions, though she decided not to mention the triple-function limb.

It now lay in disassembled parts in the waste-bin where much of it had come from in the first place.

Meanwhile, at the clinic, the plaster cast was sawn through. The top half was lifted off.

It was like opening the lid of a red casket. Hugo held his breath. He was eager to see his own familiar arm.

He saw the cotton wool lining of the cast, so soft and clean. But what was that lying in the casket?

Hugo and Patrick both gasped with horror. This didn't look like a healthy boy's arm. It didn't look like anybody's arm. It was long, thin and pale, like a hairy maggot. Patrick wondered, was this the result of that unusual potion he'd mixed?

The doctor said, "Try to wiggle your fingers, Hugo."

But Hugo's fingers were as
stiff as unused hinges. His wrist
wouldn't move either, nor his
hand or his elbow. Tears sprouted
from his eyes. His own arm was
useless. He'd almost rather have
back the triple-function limb.
It was wild but at least it was
active.

But the doctor didn't seem worried. "This is quite usual," he said. "So you're going to have to exercise it, every day. To build up those muscles. What sport d'you like?"

"I used to play football," said Hugo. "But I don't suppose they'll be wanting me back in the team, not after what happened."

"Another excellent exercise," said the doctor, "is swimming."

So on the way home, Patrick and Hugo stopped by at the municipal pool. Patrick bought a group season ticket. And quite soon the entire Spoon family had learned to swim as elegantly as a school of porpoises.

About the Author

Rachel Anderson has been a journalist but now writes books full-time. She lives in North Norfolk and in central London. She has written many books, including *Paper Faces*, for older readers, which won the *Guardian* Children's Fiction Award.

She is married with four grown-up children and several grandchildren, one of whom broke his arm and became the inspiration for this story.

Another White Wolves title
you might enjoy ...

Live the Dream!
by Jenny Oldfield

Zoey leads an ordinary life, but her secret wishes are far from normal. When she logs on to the net, she has the chance to make her wildest dreams come true. Which one will she choose?

Another White Wolves title you might enjoy ...

Swan Boy
by Diana Hendry

How did Caleb turn into a creature part boy and part swan, and come to live alone on the island of Nanna? Find out in this haunting story from a multi-prize-winning writer.

Year 3

Detective Dan • Vivian French

Buffalo Bert, the Cowboy Grandad • Michaela Morgan

Treasure at the Boot-fair • Chris Powling

Scratch and Sniff • Margaret Ryan

The Thing in the Basement • Michaela Morgan

On the Ghost-Trail • Chris Powling

Year 4

Hugo and the Long Red Arm • Rachel Anderson

Live the Dream! • Jenny Oldfield

Swan Boy • Diana Hendry

Taking Flight • Julia Green

Finding Fizz • J. Alexander

Nothing But Trouble • Alan MacDonald